I0531102

The ADVENTURES OF ScUBa Jack

The ELeMENTaL QUEEN

Written by Beth Costanzo

Illustrated by Jeremy Marks, Carlos Maldonado and

Magdalena Buslowska

JUST BECAUSE YOU CAN'T
SEE SOMETHING,

DOESN'T MEAN IT
DOESN'T EXIST!

CHAPTER 1

WHAT EVIL HAS BEEN UNLEASHED?

Lucretia was sitting on the rocks near Scuba Jack's house with Hades' chariot and horses waiting in a nearby field. Sitting on the seat was Hades' "Helmet of Invisibility." *What are the mermen from the Dragon Kingdom doing here?* Lucretia thought!

She answered her own thought aloud: "They know about the half-mermaid, half-human! Let's follow them!"

The Mermen returned to the Dragon Kingdom to relay what they had found. The mer-folk from the Dragon Kingdom could shape-shift into human form. They lived in crystal palaces guarded by ten thousand shrimp and ten thousand crabs. No mortal could enter; no mortal could find the entrance. Lucretia followed behind in her chariot without being seen. Hades' Helmet of Invisibility sure came in handy!

"Your Majesty, we have returned!" exclaimed the mermen.

"What news do you have for me?" the Dragon King replied royally.

"It is true Your Majesty! She does exist! We have seen her with our own eyes" the Mermen reported.

"What has become of her mother?" asked the Dragon King.

"Poseidon has turned her into a human!" said one of the King's scouts.

"If humans find out, we will *all* be in grave danger!" the Dragon King said frowning.

"Poseidon must understand the danger of his actions! The Elemental Queen needs to hear about this craziness! She will not be happy at all! Go to each Mermaid Kingdom and warn them about this. Each king must meet on the next full moon to discuss this situation. We will meet on the Sea Witch's Island.

"Go now to each of the ten Kingdoms!"

"Yes, Your Majesty!" replied the scouts.

CHAPTER 2

WHO STOLE THE MISSING FRUIT?

Lucretia's chariot brought her to the crystal gates of the Dragon King. Outside were ten thousand shrimp and ten thousand crabs guarding the entrance to the Kingdom. Anyone trying to enter would be overcome by these nasty little creatures that would destroy anything in their path.

How will I get in? she thought, and then she realized: *I must use the Helmet of Invisibility and walk over those icky creatures!*

"Dear chariot, hide yourself until I return! Here I go!"

"Oh, I am squishing shrimp! *Oh no, I feel crabs beneath my webbed feet! Yuck!*

Hmm, how am I going to get in this door?

I think I can fit through the bars...

I am going to take a deep breath and squeeze, squeeze, squeeze!

I'm in! I am going to walk up these stairs and find out what is going on here!"

Lucretia crept quietly down halls and up some stairs. Then she went down several sets of stairs. Next she came to a great room where the Dragon King sat. Lucretia hid behind a curtain and listened as he spoke to his soldiers.

"Hmmm, the mermaids of the world have been summoned to meet at the Sea Witch's Island on the next full moon to discuss the half-mermaid, half-human who is living in the human world. This could disrupt the balance of nature! Very interesting.........

A sea witch? thought Lucretia. *Where can I find her? It's time to go!*

Lucretia walked down several halls and somehow made her way to the basement of the castle. The air grew colder as she descended down the many stairs. It became darker; torches lit the long corridors. *What could be down here?* she wondered.

She got to the bottom of the stairs and onto a landing. The atmosphere got peculiar. Her feathers started to float upward. She walked farther into the room and noticed that the water droplets on the floor were moving up, not down.

What is this place?

Her curiosity made her walk farther into the large room. She grabbed a torch off the wall and continued to walk. She noticed a beautiful golden tree. It was not an ordinary tree—it glistened and sparkled. It was breathtaking. As she walked closer, she noticed that it was a fruit tree. Golden apples floated in the air and circled around the tree!

"I am very hungry. I am sure no one will notice
if I take just one…"

She walked closer and jumped with all her
might to reach a beautiful apple.

Just then Lucretia felt a puff of air and breathing at her back. A loud screech came from the large dragon who was summoning two other dragons who had been napping in a corner. The dragons banded together to retrieve the apple and capture the thief. Lucretia knew she needed to leave quickly and placed the Helmet of Invisibility on her head. She headed up the stairs, walked through the castle and returned to her chariot.

In another realm far, far, away a child from The Children of the Mist sat up in bed and said, "The Dragons have been awakened. The balance of the world is in grave danger!"

The Children of the Mist had dark skin with large beautiful blue eyes. Their dreams predicted the present and the future.

Meanwhile, back at the Dragon King's Castle.......

The Dragon King sat on his throne. "Your Majesty, someone has taken an apple from the Tree of Life. The dragons are in a frenzy trying to catch the thief, but he has gotten away."

"How does someone enter our kingdom and steal from the Tree of Life without being seen? It is impossible!"

"Send out word to all the Elemental Kingdoms about our missing fruit. Ask them to aid us in our need!"

"Prepare a letter to the Elemental Queen and ask her to meet me in my chambers."

"Your Majesty, she never meets with anyone! I don't think she will come!" the soldier replied.

"Tell the Elemental Queen that one of our fruits from the Tree of Life is missing! If it gets into the wrong hands, the world as we know it will change because the balance of nature will be off. That means evil will become more powerful unless the fruit is returned and the balance is restored. She will come!" said the King.

chaPTER 3
WORLD DoMiNaTiON

The clouds moved in and the ocean became angry. The wind grew stronger as the waves crashed into the shore.

"Wow, the weather has changed quickly!" Scuba Jack noticed.

"The air feels different. I don't think this is a typical storm! Something is wrong! I can feel it" said Sahri.

"What do you mean?" Scuba Jack asked.

"I am scared, Jack! Something bad is coming!" Sahri exclaimed.

Nearby, Lucretia was sitting with the golden apple. It shimmered and sparkled and drew Lucretia to it. It made her even more evil than she had been as Hades' sidekick.

"It's surely a magical fruit. I need to protect it. I must call upon all the birds of the air and sea to help me."

Just then a sparrow landed next to Lucretia.

"Dear Sparrow, go tell the birds of the world that I need their help. I have something valuable that they have only heard about in fairy tales. They will marvel at its beauty. They must all come and see it. We birds will become more powerful than gods with what I have in my possession."

Then Lucretia got an idea. "I am going to place the apple in the water and summon the undead. It's worth a try. I need all the help that I can get!"

"Dear spirits of the sea,

Please hear my plea—

Send all the undead souls,

Please send them here to me!

The earth shook, the water got rough, and the waves became huge. Just then a pirate ship lifted from the deep, then another and another. Within minutes, twenty ships sat before Lucretia awaiting her command.

"Dear pirates, please wait patiently until I am done with these silly birds!" Lucretia bellowed.

(Undead pirates basically do what they are told because they don't have brains; they just love to scare people and wreak havoc on everyone in their paths.)

"I am going to be more powerful than a god!" Lucretia cackled.

Birds started to fly in to see the treasure. Hawks, eagles, pelicans, crows, falcons all came to view Lucretia's fabulous treasure. Within twenty minutes more than one hundred thousand birds stood before her.

The King of the Crows stood next to Lucretia and inquired, "Why have you called us here? Don't you realize we have better things to do?

"In due time my friend, in due time!" Lucretia responded in a stern voice.

"Dear friends, what I have here can make our kind the most powerful in the entire world. What I have, no one has ever seen, but only heard about in fairy tales."

"If I don't see it now, I am leaving!" yelled the Crow King.

Lucretia pulled out the golden apple and raised it above her head.

"It is true!" shouted the Crow King.

All the birds bowed to its presence.

"Where did you get that?" the King asked.

"In the castle of the Dragon Kings," Lucretia shouted.

"You stole it? Everyone will be looking for it! Great evil will enter the world. The balance of nature will be gone!" the Crow King exclaimed nervously.

"They will never find it! I can make it invisible! Not to mention, I can use this—or shall I say— *we* can use this to our advantage."

"Why should we trust you? You have been in the Underworld for many years and it has affected your brain! " said the King.

"Hades was good to me and taught me many things! The most important lesson was to take advantage of every situation that comes your way!" Lucretia shouted.

"What's in it for us?" the King inquired.

"Oh, just the usual……power, wealth, the world."

"And you intend to share this with all of us?" the King said suspiciously.

Lucretia crossed her toes, crossed her wings and then, with an evil grin said, "Of course I will!"

CHAPTER 4

THE FAIRIES WILL HELP!

Falhurst stopped by Scuba Jack's and Sahri's house.

"Hey, Falhurst," said Scuba Jack.

"Good morning, Jack!" said Falhurst.

"What on earth is up with this weather?" Jack asked.

"Something peculiar, for sure. The air feels heavy. Ardith should be here any minute to explain. How is little Jewel doing?"

"Well, she keeps eating all of the family pets, but other than that, she is just perfect! Thankfully, she looks like her mother!" Jack smiled.

Sahri walked onto the dock. "Hello, Falhurst. I sense Ardith is almost here?"

Just then Ardith swam up to the dock.

"Can you feel the difference in the air and wind? Someone or something stole a sacred fruit from the Dragon King's castle" Ardith cried.

"Say what? Who is the Dragon King? What kind of fruit?" Jack asked.

Ardith explained, "The dragons protect the balance of nature by protecting the Tree of Life. If one of its fruits is missing, the balance of the universe is in jeopardy. Evil can become stronger and disaster can occur at every moment.

Falhurst wondered, "How did anyone get past the Dragons?"

"Their cries were heard throughout the Mermaid Kingdoms. A meeting has been called by the Dragon King. The Kings of each Mermaid Kingdom will be attending," said Ardith.

"When will this meeting occur?" Falhurst asked.

"It will occur on the next full moon. I don't know the location. It's a secret! But, I have some bad news for Scuba Jack and Sahri.............."

"What's wrong, Ardith?" Sahri asked.

"The meeting was called because of Jewel. The mermaids found out she exists. Jewel, being half mermaid and half human, can put us all in danger. If humans find out, we can all be destroyed, although the missing fruit has taken precedence for the moment! " Ardith explained.

"I need to know where the meeting is! I need to attend and defend my daughter!" Scuba Jack shouted.

"They do not want humans at the meeting! But if you just happen to show up and plead your case, they might listen!" Falhurst offered.

"Ardith, please help me! I don't want them to take my baby away or Sahri!" pleaded Jack.

"Well, Jack, you do have two advantages--the book and the wand! The only ones who can or may help you are in the Elemental Realms," Ardith responded.

"The Elemental Realms? What is that?" asked Jack

"Elementals are Earth Spirits who rule over the flowers, plants, trees, soil, rocks, stones, crystals and all living beings," explained Sahri.

Falhurst added, "The Elementals live among the plants, water and animals. One of the reasons we feel so good when we are around nature is because of these powerful healing spirits. There are many different types of beings in the Elemental Kingdom, including mythical creatures—leprechauns, elves, fairies, sylphs, mermaids, and tree people. Elementals create abundance and balance on the earth and must be respected and appreciated."

Six crows sat around the dock listening to the conversation.

"I don't know why, but I feel like I'm being watched," said Scuba Jack.

"Evil grows more powerful by the hour. That's what you're feeling!" Ardith retorted.

"How can I speak with the fairies?" Jack asked Falhurst.

"Well, it isn't that easy," said Ardith

"I know. Remember? I had to ask some trees for their wood to make a wand? My bum hasn't been the same since!" exclaimed Jack.

"You must go deep into the woods and find a circle of mushrooms. Within that circle you must leave an offering for the fairies. If they like you and your offering, they will speak with you!"

"What should I leave?" asked Jack

"Flowers, berries or anything from nature," replied Ardith.

"It's done! I will leave in the morning!" bravely said Jack.

"You have three days until the full moon!" announced Falhurst.

Chapter 5

A Circle of Mushrooms and an Offering of Flowers!

The next morning Scuba Jack woke up and headed into the forest. He walked for miles looking for a circle of mushrooms. He searched and searched and was about to give up when it happened. He walked into a clearing. The sun sparkled through the trees. A waterfall made the most beautiful sound. The breeze had a lovely floral scent that made him happy with each breath. It was a magical place. There by the waterfall was a circle of mushrooms. It was just as he had been told, only better. He bent down and placed a bouquet of flowers in the center and left.

The next morning he got up and decided to use the Starlink to arrive at the circle of mushrooms.

This time he sat by the mushroom circle and he placed a bunch of grapes inside. He looked sad, really sad. He began to tear up!

"I know that you don't know me. I know that my problems aren't yours, but I have a beautiful baby girl who means everything to her mother and me. It doesn't matter that she eats all the goldfish in the bowl, or chatters like a dolphin. I was bestowed the best gift anyone could ever receive in the world. My wife Sahri was turned from a mermaid into a human so she could be with me. Our daughter is half mermaid and half human, but she is only a baby. I love her and her mother so much! I can't imagine my life without them. Please, if anyone is listening, please help me."

A tear rolled down his cheek.

He started to stand up to leave but then noticed a small glowing light coming toward him. As the light got closer, Scuba Jack recognized that it was a Fairy. He wiped his cheek. A big smile appeared on his face.

A fairy with fluttering wings as fast as a hummingbird's looked lovingly into Scuba Jack's eyes.

She was the most beautiful fairy imaginable.
Then, in a kind voice, she spoke to Scuba
Jack. "Hello, I am Aurora of the Fairy Realm.
We have heard your plea for help, and we have
heard about you and your daughter. We also
know that you have Hades' Spell Book and a
magic wand. You have helped mankind and all
the Elemental Kingdoms with your bravery. We
would be glad to help you! What do you need,
Scuba Jack?"

"Wow, you know my name?"

"Of course we do! The trees, flowers, wind, and
animals all whisper to us what is happening in
the universe!"

"The Mermaid Kings and Queens are meeting on the next full moon to discuss my daughter. I would like to be there and defend my family. Please help me!" Jack pleaded.

Aurora placed her tiny hand on his forehead and sang a quiet song:

When the moon is full at night,

When a shooting star takes flight,

Twirl your dress and wave your wand,

Sing a lovely fairy song

Flickering lights beneath the dew,

Lovely, fragrant flowers of blue,

Dappled in the earth's twilight,

With gossamer wings they take flight.

Tranquil pleasures, laughter, love.

Celestial bodies from above,

Each cave and hollow has a way,

To enchanted places where fairies stay.

Enter in and you'll transcend,

Nature's beauty and all its friends,

Whisper peaceful songs of love,

Sent from the stars and heaven above!

Their lighted globes are seen at night.

Love and laughter give delight.

Make a wish and hold it tight,

Hope and believe with all your might—

Then just maybe on this quiet night,

All your dreams and wishes will take

flight!

Scuba Jack felt a peaceful calm come over him as hundreds of fairies descended around him. He wasn't worried anymore, and he didn't feel sad. He was now ready to meet the Kings and convince them that everything was going to be fine.

"They are all meeting at Sea Witch's Island, Jack. The full moon will be in two days, so you must be ready. Someone has stolen the golden apple from the tree of life. The balance of nature is in jeopardy."

"Maybe I could help bring back the golden apple?" Jack said.

"Be careful! The Sea Witch can be deadly. She has great magic. Some say it is black magic," said Aurora nervously.

"Why would the Mermaid Kings associate themselves with someone who uses black magic?" asked Jack.

"She is powerful and can see the future! And she sends the Elemental Queen fairies who help her. She has been helpful to the queen."

"Her island is located just past the Haunted Bacchus Forest," Aurora reported.

"That is a little scary, Aurora, but I will just zap myself there," said Jack.

"Good luck, Jack! Be safe!" begged Aurora.

"Thank you so much!" Jack replied.

He pushed the button and was gone.

CHAPTER 6
THE CROWS ARE MULTIPLYING

Scuba Jack was transported to his favorite chair on the dock. He noticed hundreds of crows perched around his dock!

"What is going on here?" he ye led.

Paco landed next to him and said, "Hello, Scuba Jack! Notice anything peculiar?

"Well, as a matter of fact, I do!" answered Scuba Jack.

"The birds of the world have been summoned for a meeting."

"Why?"

"Apparently, a crazy, evil bird named Lucretia wants to dominate the universe. Blah, blah, blah!"

"Does this have anything to do with the missing golden apple?" asked Jack.

"Yes, Lucretia was Hades' number one evil-doer in the underworld and wants to rule the world," exclaimed Paco.

"Is Hades at it again?" asked Jack.

"No, Lucretia's evil scheming has nothing to do with Hades."

"Hmmmmm. I need to get that apple back!"

"But how, Scuba Jack?" asked Paco.

"I'm not sure! But I know someone who can help," said Jack

"Who?" said Paco.

"The Spell Casters!" said Scuba Jack.

CHAPTER 7
THE SPELL CASTERS

Professor Galaxy stopped by the dock for a visit.

"Hey, Scuba Jack! Ominous weather we're having, huh?"

"Well, it's not ordinary weather, Professor, that's for sure," Scuba Jack replied.

Scuba Jack explained all the events that had taken place, especially the discovery of his daughter being half-mermaid and half-human.

"But Jewel is just a baby. What harm could she do?" asked Professor Galaxy.

"The mermaids are afraid that if she is discovered by the humans, then all mermaids could be found and destroyed. I am on my way to see the Spell Casters. I need to find the missing golden apple."

Professor Galaxy asked, "May I join you? You never know what you'll see deep beneath the ground!"

"Sure!" Scuba Jack responded. "Let's go!"

Pop! Scuba Jack and Professor Galaxy were transported to the Spell Casters' Kingdom.

"Ring the bell, Professor!"

"Who is it?" said the Spell Caster.

"It's Scuba Jack! I need to talk to you!"

The thirty latches unlocked one by one…

"Hello, Scuba Jack!" Bob exclaimed.

"Well, hello Bob! How was Brazil?"

"We all had a wonderful time! Thank you for that! I didn't think Hades was going to keep his promise, but I'm glad you did!"

"I need some advice, Bob."

"Sure. What is it, Scuba Jack? Oh, wait, we love this part of our day where we get to foresee your question. Let me call the rest of the boys!"

Moments later, the Spell Casters entered the room. All of them raised their hands in the air.

A vision appeared on the wall: it was Lucretia with the golden apple.

"The golden apple is under the Helmet of Invisibility. This will be difficult for you Scuba Jack. Did you know that every realm has a golden apple for safe keeping? They are hidden throughout the world."

"No, I didn't. Why?" Jack asked.

"Each apple fits into a Dragon's Seal. The seal opens a door," answered Bob

"What's inside the door?" Jack asked.

Dragon eggs!" said Bob

"Dragon eggs?" replied Jack.

"Yes, they are only hatched when the world is in dire need!" Bob explained. "The apples will be found in the seven wonders of the world."

"The seven wonders of the world?" exclaimed Jack. "Where do I begin?"

"Stonehenge, then the Coliseum in Rome, Great Wall of China, Statue of Liberty, The Great Pyramid. I don't know.......... look on the internet! You must look for a golden apple at each site. Each apple will fit into the Dragon's Seal," Bob explained.

"Where is the Seal located?" asked Jack.

"I'm not sure, but we'll help you along the way. I promise!" Bob said. "I must go and see the Elemental Queen."

"Oh, the Elemental Queen.....I thought she didn't like visitors?" asked Jack.

"Well, she likes me, but I must convince her that the fate of the universe depends on her cooperation."

"Don't worry, Scuba Jack, I'll go with you," the Professor said.

"But before I visit the Queen, I am going to enter our watermelon eating contest"

With the touch of a button, Scuɔa Jack and the
Professor were gone.

CHAPTER 8

CHILDREN
OF THE MIST

Scuba Jack and Professor Galaxy found themselves in a forest standing in an eerie, thick mist.

"Where are we, Professor?" asked Scuba Jack.

"I'm not sure! I think the Starlink malfunctioned again!"

Three children walked forward from the mist.

"Hello! We are the Children from the Mist. We can see the future through our dreams."

"It's nice to meet you" Scuba Jack said nervously.

One of the children continued, "We need to speak with you because you are in grave danger. Mankind as we know it is in jeopardy. You are beginning a quest for the golden apples. Be careful, Scuba Jack. There are those who will try to stop you. Lucretia has gathered an army that is more powerful than Hades. The golden apple increases her powers and casts a spell on all that place their eyes upon it. It is like a trance, and they will do anything to protect it. Your friend Paco will fall madly in love with Lucretia and he will help her and turn against you."

"But, Paco is my best friend!" Scuba Jack exclaimed.

"He was, but when you were learning magic from the Spell Casters, you placed a spell on Paco, correct? Do you remember this? Scuba Jack?"

You said Paco would fall in love with the first pelican he saw," the Professor reminded him.

"So, the first pelican is Lucretia? No, it can't be!" Jack said sadly.

"Yes, I am sorry, but it is true," replied one of the children.

"She wields evil from the air, water, fire, and the Underworld"

"What you seek is the Dragon's seal. Long ago seven golden apples were placed in the seven Wonders of the World. When you find the apples, place them in the Dragon's seal. The Dragon's Seal will open the door to the Eighth wonder of the world. Return the Eighth Wonder of the World to the Dragon King. Your Spell Book will help you! This is your only chance to stop all the evil and chaos in the world.

"But, where do I find the Dragon's Seal?"

"Clues will be left where you find the golden apples. Lucretia's powers are strengthening."

"The Eighth Wonder of the World is dragon eggs, right?" said Scuba Jack.

"Yes. But be careful not to drop or disturb them. They must be nurtured within the Dragon King's castle," said another child.

"You must go now! You have much to do and the full moon is in two days!"

"Thank you for giving me this information."

"Be careful and trust no one. Remain true to yourself, Scuba Jack and Professor. You will be tempted with riches beyond your wildest dreams!" said another child.

"We will!" answered the Professor.

Pop! They were gone!

CHAPTER 9

LOCUSTS ARE EVERYWHERE!

Professor Galaxy and Scuba Jack were transported to Jack's house. Sahri came outside to greet them.

She gave Scuba Jack a big hug and kiss. "I missed you, my love. Where have you been?"

"We were trying to get the golden apple back, but we met some children who walked from a thick mist and told us how to stop Lucretia and her army.

"Children?" Sahri asked.

"They were so beautiful and had big beautiful blue eyes. They said their dreams predict the future," Jack explained.

"Oh, you met the *Children of the Mist*. I have only heard about them, but have never seen them."

"They told us to visit some major landmarks and there we would find the seven golden apples. Is it my imagination, Sahri, or are there more crows here? I don't want to leave you and Jewel here alone."

"Don't worry, my love. I still have all my senses and can tell when I'm in danger. If I need help, I will call upon the mermaids. It's time for you to save the world again."

Just then a seventy mile long twister tore into Majestic Harbor without warning. It rearranged the lives of everyone who crossed its path. The tornado caused automobiles to become airborne and ripped homes to shreds. The flying debris was tossed about in the wind and turned broken glass and other debris into lethal missiles.

Just in……. News Report, Channel 12 NEWS!!!

Locusts are buzzing all over Majestic Harbor. Thousands of locusts…. everywhere the eye can see, eating almost everything in sight. Stay inside and avoid contact.

Another news station was reporting earthquakes elsewhere in the world. The tremors generated a tsunami and set off multiple landslides, severing power from the area impacted by the quake.

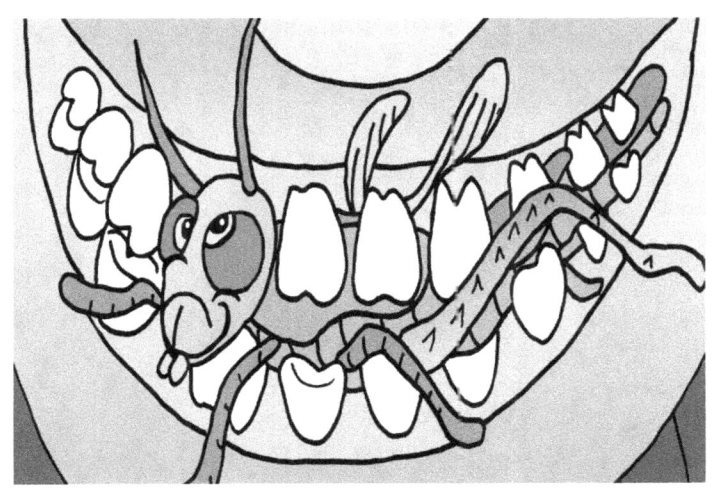

"I think I have bugs in my teeth," Scuba Jack groused.

"Scuba Jack, hit the button! I can't hold on much longer!" Professor Galaxy cried.

Pop! They were gone!

CHAPTER 10

LET'S FIND
THOSE GOLDEN EGGS!

Scuba Jack and the Professor used the Starlink to get to the Professor's lab where they searched on the computer for the seven Wonders of the World.

"Scuba Jack, the computer lists many Wonders of the World," the Professor said.

"Well, we need to visit the top seven," said Scuba Jack.

"Let's start with Stonehenge. It is located in Wiltshire, United Kingdom."

"Sounds good! Let's go!" *Zap*! They were gone!

Stonehenge

"Wow, this is amazing! There are a lot of tourists here," said Scuba Jack.

"This is one of the most famous sites in the world. Stonehenge is the remains of a ring of standing stones. Archaeologists believe it was built anywhere from 3000 BC to 2000 BC. Stonehenge is believed to be a burial place."

Scuba Jack opened the Spell Book and began turning the pages, looking for the perfect spell.

"I found it! Here we go! It says to say this three times!

> "Keeper of what disappears,
> Hear me now -- open your ears.
> Find for me what I now seek,
> By Moon, Sun, Earth, Air, Fire and Sea.
>
> Find the golden apple."

Suddenly Scuba Jack was pulled toward one of the rocks. His hands began to dig uncontrollably. One foot under the ground he found something wrapped in an old cloth. He opened the cloth.

"Bingo! We got it!" The golden apple was wrapped in a cloth and had a number on it. The number was forty-three.

"Hmm, I think it is a clue, Scuba Jack!" the Professor exclaimed. "What is our next location?"

The Great Pyramid of Giza!

They hit the button and were gone!

The Great Pyramid of Giza

"Wow, this is quite a sandstorm!" the Professor marveled.

"Blah! Blah! I think I got some sand in my mouth!" Scuba Jack mumbled in reply.

"Here goes the spell........

Keeper of what disappears,
Hear me now -- open your ears.
Find for me what I now seek,
By Moon, Sun, Earth, Air, Fire and Sea.
Find the golden apple."

Just then a camel walked by and let out a large snort that made Scuba Jack jump!

"Geesh, it's not very friendly here!" he said.

"The Great Pyramid of Giza was built for the Pharaoh Khufu. Egyptologists believe the pyramid was built as a tomb over a ten to twenty year period ending around 2560 B.C.," explained Professor Galaxy.

Just then, Scuba Jack's legs began to move like they had a mind of their own—he couldn't control them. People visiting the pyramid started to move away from Scuba Jack, thinking that he had lost his marbles. Then, like a shot, he ran to the back of the pyramid, bent over and began to dig. He quickly noticed a nob and turned it. Out rolled another apple wrapped in a cloth. Another number was written on the cloth.

"Another clue, I suspect," the Professor guessed.

"What's our next destination?"

"Christ the Redeemer in Brazil," the Professor replied. "Shall I do the honors?"

"Yes, please. Press the button and zap us to Brazil!"

Zap! They were gone!

Christ the Redeemer

"Wow, this monument is huge!" Scuba Jack said in awe. It was created by French sculptor Paul Landowski and built by Brazilian engineer Heitor da Silva Costa in collaboration with French engineer Albert Caquot. We are at the Peak of Corcovado Mountain, in the Tijuca Forest National Park overlooking the beautiful city of Rio. This is a symbol of Brazilian Christianity. This monument is ninety-eight feet tall, not including a twenty-six foot pedestal," Professor Galaxy informed Scuba Jack.

"The Spell Casters love Brazil and got a nice two week vacation!" Scuba Jack exclaimed.

"I can see why they liked it—sun, beaches and beautiful bikinis...ugh, I mean girls. Um, let's get started, Scuba Jack. Recite the spell," Professor Galaxy said nervously.

> "Keeper of what disappears,
> Hear me now -- open your ears.
> Find for me what I now seek,
> By Moon, Sun, Earth, Air, Fire and Sea.
> Find the golden apple."

Once again, Scuba Jack began to move uncontrollably, but this time he was doing pirouettes like a ballerina. All he needed was a tutu and he would have been ready for the ballet. It was quite embarrassing, but it led him to their destination.

A small hole lay beneath the structure. Scuba Jack reached in and pulled out a small angry mouse. He scurried away and angrily looked at Scuba Jack, as if to say "You disturbed my afternoon nap." Again, he reached in and pulled out another golden apple wrapped in a cloth with a number on it.

"That's three apples. Four more to go! What's our next destination, Professor?

"The Golden Gate Bridge in San Francisco."

"Great! Let's go!" Scuba Jack replied.

Poof! They were gone!

The Golden Gate Bridge

"Wow! This is a big bridge!" Scuba Jack cried. It is a suspension bridge three miles long. It links San Francisco to Marin County. "Say the spell and let's see what happens," Professor Galaxy prodded.

"Ok here goes!" Scuba Jack again recited the spell.

Scuba Jack began to cartwheel and handspring down the bridge. His tumbling was as good as a gymnast in the Olympics. It was incredible to watch. People driving by began to clap. Who knew Scuba Jack had that kind of talent?

He tumbled off the end of the bridge where the pavement met the dirt and once again began to dig. He dug deeper than ever before. Eventually he pulled out the same type cloth with a golden apple inside. Once again, a number was written on the cloth.

"Ok what's our next destination, Professor?"

"The Great Wall of China, in Beijing!" the Professor replied.

In the blink of an eye, they were gone!

Great Wall of China

The two were transported to the Great Wall.
An old lady was having difficulty crossing it.
Professor Galaxy walked up to her and took
her by the arm. The old woman responded, "I
am fine, young man!"

"Don't be silly, I would love to help you!" he
responded.

"I said, I don't need your help!'" she insisted.

Just then the old woman's face turned into that
of a hideous witch.

"Well, OK.....Gotta go!" the Professor replied.

Scuba Jack said, "We don't have time to fool
around, Professor! The full moon is coming.

Scuba Jack started reciting the spell, completely ignoring the Professor. The world needed him and he was in the "Scuba Jack zone." Nothing was going to stop him now.

Just as before, Scuba Jack began to move. This time he wasn't tumbling like an Olympic Champion, or dancing like a ballerina. He was moving like a Ninja. He jumped on the wall then down, then flipped and landed in a "ready for battle" stance. He turned and faced the wall, then tapped on one of the stones. Out fell a golden apple wrapped in a cloth with a number written on the cloth.

"Our next destination, please?" asked Scuba Jack.

"The Statue of Liberty in New York!" the Professor said.

Statue of Liberty

"Wow, just think! Some of our relatives may have come through here to start their new lives," Scuba Jack said with wonder.

"On October 28, 1886, the Statue of Liberty was a gift of friendship from the people of France to the United States. This gift was given to commemorate the centennial of the American Declaration of Independence. The Statue of Liberty has become an icon that represents democracy, independence and freedom to the American people," gloated Professor Galaxy, who thought he was such a smarty pants!

"I know. It's amazing! But we need to find the next apple—FAST! Where's the spell book, Professor? Ok here goes!"

> "Keeper of what disappears,
> Hear me now -- open your ears.
> Find for me what I now seek,
> By Moon, Sun, Earth, Air, Fire
> and Sea.
>
> Find the golden apple."

Scuba Jack's legs began to move like he was dancing an Irish jig. People began to throw coins at his feet thinking he was a street performer. The Professor began to collect all the money Scuba Jack earned. Just then a swarm of crows began to dive at the duo.

"What's going on?" asked Scuba Jack, ducking every which way to avoid being pecked by the angry flock.

"I suspect this is Lucretia's evil army of smelly birds!" the Professor answered, ducking and scowling.

"Quick, let's get inside!"

They jumped in the elevator and headed for the crown of Lady Liberty!

When the door opened, Scuba Jack walked to the window and opened it.

"The Statue of Liberty crown actually consists of seven spikes that represent the seven continents and oceans on this planet," the Professor continued.

Scuba Jack climbed out and began to climb one of the spikes. Again the crows dive-bombed him. They knew what he was looking for and didn't want him to find it. One of the crows almost knocked him off, but Scuba Jack quickly grabbed on tightly. Then he saw the cloth-wrapped apple tucked on a shelf on the backside of the spike. He reached out as far as he could and finally grabbed the apple. The crows kept tugging on his wetsuit and his hair. They even pooped on his head! He placed the wrapped apple securely in hand, went back through the window and wiped the poop from his forehead.

"I can tell that crow had fish for lunch! I can distinctly smell fish! Oh, that's disgusting!

"What's our next destination, Professor?"

"The Coliseum in Rome, Scuba Jack!"

Zap! They were gone!

The Coliseum in Rome

"Here we are at the Coliseum in Rome, Italy. Construction began under Emperor Vespasian in 70 AD, and was completed in 80 AD under his successor and heir Titus. The Coliseum could hold fifty thousand to eighty thousand spectators and was used for gladiator contests, mock sea battles, animal hunts, executions, re-enactments of famous battles, and dramas based on mythology," the Professor explained.

"Let me see the spell book!" Jack requested.

"Keeper of what disappears,
Hear me now -- open your ears.
Find for me what I now seek,
By Moon, Sun, Earth, Air, Fire and Sea.

Find the golden apple."

Just then the ghostly figure of a gladiator appeared before Scuba Jack and the Professor. He drew his sword preparing for battle.

"PROFESSOR!!!!!" Scuba Jack gulped.

Scuba Jack kicked a stone. It rolled to the ground. He grabbed the last apple and said quickly, "OK, our last destination is Lucretia's feathery lair! Let's go!"

Zap! They were gone!

CHAPTER 11

LUCRETIA'S FEATHERY LAIR

"Wow! Look at all these birds! We are going to need to fit in. We'll need some feathers or bird suits."

Scuba Jack took the wand from the Professor's pocket and tapped it twice. *Poof!* They both suddenly looked like large, colorful parrots. Each began to squawk like parrots to blend in. They noticed Lucretia sitting up high in a large bird nest. As they got closer they noticed that the Helmut of Invisibility was s tting next to her.

"Do I know you? Where are you from?" Lucretia asked.

"We're from the Amazon! You know what they say….Everything is bigger in the Amazon!"

"Yes, that is true! We have awakened bats from the Amazon. They are seven feet tall and have been asleep for thousands of years. They will make me more powerful! The world will be mine, all mine!" Lucretia declared with an evil look in her eye.

Just then Professor's cell phone rang.

"WHAT IS THAT NOISE?" Lucretia thundered.

"It's not me. I think it's that ostrich wearing the ninja headband," said the Professor, lying through his teeth.

Just then two emus escorted the ostrich to a nest where they could keep a watchful eye on him.

The Professor turned, pulled out his phone and whispered, "Hey Paco, I can't talk right now-- I am with that evil pelican, Lucretia! Gotta go!"

"We want to join your army!" said Scuba Jack. "We want to help you become more powerful! We can get all our parrot relatives from the Amazon to come here and help you become Queen of the World!"

"They are already here! Let me summon them so you can say hi!"

Lucretia looked at one of the turkeys and said, "You.....get the parrots from the Amazon!"

Scuba Jack began to speak pig Latin to the Professor. "We etterbay et outta eh, NOW-eh!"

The Amazon parrots flew in. "My lady, you called for us?"

"Yes! Here are your relatives from the Amazon!"

"My lady, I do not know these parrots!"

Just then Scuba Jack let out a loud sneeze. The fake beak flew right off his nose!

"Imposters!" Lucretia shrieked. "Get them!"

Scuba Jack leaped through the air in slow motion, just like something you see in a ninja movie. He grabbed the Helmut. Underneath was an apple wrapped in cloth.

Scuba Jack and the Professor fled from the birds until they came to the edge of a cliff. Below the cliff was the ocean. In it were dozens of hungry sharks waiting for their next meal.

"Ha, ha, ha!" Lucretia laughed. "Below are sharks waiting for the scraps of fish that we throw them each hour. I am sure they would love to taste the likes of you!"

The birds began to crowd in on the two men in bird suits. Scuba Jack and the Professor were on the very edge, fearing the worst, when they saw the holograph-like face of Bob the Spell Caster hovering above their heads.

"Don't worry! Just jump!" Bob directed.

"You want us to jump? Are you crazy?" Scuba Jack inquired nervously.

"Just trust! I told you I would help you along the way!" Bob affirmed.

Scuba Jack grabbed the Professor's hand. They both jumped, yelling, "Geronimo!"

A hippocampi spiraled out of the water. Jack and the Professor landed nicely on her back. Mermaids suddenly appeared to help fight off the sharks. The two escaped safely.

When all the excitement was over, Paco arrived and accidently walked right up to Lucretia. His eyes met hers. It was love at first sight for Paco. Fireworks went off in his head.

Scuba Jack had learned how to cast spells with the help of his magic wand. As a student of the Spell Casters, he learned to place a love spell on one of his best friends; Paco the pelican. Unfortunately, Paco fell in love with the first bird he saw: the most evil bird in history, Lucretia!

"Love is in the air!" Paco sang.

"What did you say?" Lucretia asked.

"Um, a dove is flying over there!" Paco replied.

"Yes, doves are everywhere!" the puzzled Lucretia agreed. "Come with me. You can be of great help!" said Lucretia.

"Ok my little flower! Oh, um, yes, indeed, you of great power!" the smitten Paco replied.

Chapter 12
Back To The Lab!

"Let's see what happens when I put these numbers into the computer…" the Professor muttered.

"What's happening?" Jack prompted after about fifteen seconds.

"It's analyzing the data and looking at all the possible ways these numbers can go together! This computer has had some enhancements to make it able to decipher scientific data quickly. Here we go…"

After a few more seconds, he added, "It looks like …perhaps…coordinates on a map…

These are the coordinates of Mt. Rushmore!

Black Hill National Forest

13024 South Dakota 244

Keystone, SD 57751

Looks like the seal is located in Mt. Rushmore! Let's gather the apples and be on our way!"

CHAPTER 13
MT. RUSHMORE

"The Mount Rushmore National Memorial is a sculpture carved into the granite face of Mount Rushmore (Lakota Sioux name: Six Grandfathers). It was sculpted by Danish-American Gutzon Borglum and his son, Lincoln Borglum. Mount Rushmore features sixty foot sculptures of the heads of four United States presidents: George Washington, Thomas Jefferson, Theodore Roosevelt, and Abraham Lincoln," Professor Galaxy advised upon their arrival.

Scuba Jack took out his Spell Book and began to recite the spell for the last time. There was a horse tied to a post in front of the monument so the Professor and Scuba Jack hopped on and rode to the back of the monument. On the back of the monument was a medium-size locked door behind some large bushes.

"Now what are we going to do?" Scuba Jack asked.

"Lucky for you I brought the wand!" the Professor smiled.

"Hey, what are you two doing? You took my horse!" a park ranger called out as he approached them.

Scuba Jack looked at the park ranger, pointed the wand at him and ordered, "Freeze!"

The park ranger froze. Next, Scuba jack pointed the wand at the lock and said, "Open!" The door swung open. Inside it was the Golden Seal. It was beautiful! It had gold carvings of dragons on it. Scuba Jack and the Professor carefully placed the apples in the holes of the seal. The seal opened slowly. A mist poured out and an orange glow became visible from inside. There positioned on three pedestals were the three beautiful dragon eggs.

"They're magnificent!" Scuba Jack exclaimed.

"We need to be careful," the Professor warned. "Don't break the eggs! They're crucial if we want to save the world."

"Next stop: the Dragon King's castle!" Scuba Jack announced.

"Um, but first, Scuba Jack, you should un-freeze the nice park ranger" the Professor reminded.

"Un-freeze!" Scuba Jack commanded.

"You boys need to come with me!" he told them.

Poof! They were gone!

"Where in Sam Hill did they go?" the ranger said, looking around. Unable to figure it out, he said to himself, "I think I need a vacation…"

CHAPTER 14
DRAGON KINGS

"Wow, this castle is magnificent. But eew, look at all those crabs and shrimp! There are millions of them! What are we going to do?" Scuba Jack asked.

"We are going to run as fast as we can and get through that front door!" the Professor responded.

"Ok, let's do this! RUN! Eew, Eew, Eew! These crabs are squishy! One grabbed my........Ow, ow, ow, ow!"

They reached the door and banged on it hard.

C---R---E---A---K! The door slowly opened. They walked down a dimly-lit hallway into an area with a pool and a throne on which the Dragon King sat.

"Hello! We've been expecting you! Do you have the eggs?" asked the Dragon King.

"Yes, we do. your Majesty!" answered the Professor.

A bright golden glow entered the room announcing the arrival of the most beautiful women the two had ever seen: The Elemental Queen.

"Hello! I am the Elemental Queen. I rule over all the Elementals of the planet. The dragons will help save the planet, but first you must go home and help your family. I will call upon you soon."

Just then three dragons entered the room. Fire shot from their nostrils. All at once the dragons blew enough warmth to warm the eggs.

"Farewell, Scuba Jack!" said the Elemental Queen.

Poof! They were gone.

CHAPTER 15
THE 11ᵀʰ CHOIR

An old man approached Scuba Jack and asked, "Hey there young fellow! Why are you looking so sad?"

"Well, I have a lot on my mind." Scuba Jack replied.

"Sometimes things aren't as bad as they seem," the old man suggested.

"Well, with all due respect, sir……I can assure you, they are!" Scuba Jack responded.

"Just because you can't see something, doesn't mean it doesn't exist," responded the old man.

"Believe me, I know first-hand all about that!" curtly added Scuba Jack.

"Everything is going to be fine. You just wait and see. You have more friends than you know," the old man declared with kindness.

Scuba Jack started becoming anxious. The full moon would appear in just a few hours.

"I'm sorry! I have a lot to do, and not a lot of time to do it! It was great to meet you! I'm sorry. What's your name?" said Scuba Jack

"My name is Clement, but you can call me Clem."

"It was great to meet you, Clem! Really, I must go now!"

"Watch out for Odessa! Her magic is powerful! Some say she dabbles in black magic!"

"How did you know that?" Scuba Jack asked.

"My kind is called many things, but mostly The Watchers, the Grigori or the 11th Choir. We are acutely attuned to the symphony of the planet and hear disturbances that no one else can hear. We intervene when necessary. If a demon assaults a human in his dreams, a Watcher can hear it. If an angel makes a baby cry, a Watcher can hear it. If someone gets stranded on the side of the road, we offer our assistance and call the police. Your situation has caught our attention. We have been following you for quite some time. Don't worry, there are many ready to lend a hand as needed. The Spell Casters are also our friends. We all work together for the Betterment of Mankind," Clement explained.

"So, you're like the magical police?"

"Well, yes, sort of. We have been watching over entire generations for more than ten thousand years. We can see an individual's entire family tree, going up or down a number of generations. We can tell if an individual is destined to have a descendant with an unusually important destiny. We even have details about the predestined one. You, Scuba Jack, are a chosen one!"

Scuba Jack replied, "Yes, I have heard that before. This is my second time saving the universe! Don't worry, I will be careful!"

With the press of a button, Scuba Jack was gone.

CHAPTER 16
FOSSEGRIM

Scuba Jack's young daughter Jewel Daisy sat on a dock while her mother was tidying up their house. Suddenly an incredibly handsome young man appeared at the end of the dock. He was dressed in a dark suit and was playing the most beautiful music on his violin. Jewel crawled to the end of the dock to be nearer to the man. His song was enchanting. The toddler was mesmerized as she sat next to him.

Sahri felt a jolt of fear and sensed something was wrong. She ran out of the house to check on Jewel and noticed her daughter sitting next to the young man. Her senses told her that he wasn't an ordinary person—he was a Fossegrim—and she knew he was trying to lure Jewel to her death at the bottom of the sea.

"Jewel, crawl to Mommy!" Sahri beckoned frantically, hoping not to scare her with her own fright.

The Fossegrim pointed to the water and made a large circular motion with his finger. Immediately a large whirlpool began to form. He pointed to Sahri and then to the water.

Sahri was thrown into the air and sucked into the whirlpool.

A male mermaid who was patrolling the area noticed the Fossegrim and summoned other mermaids to help. Sahri's sister Sanna, who was also in the area, dove straight into the whirlpool, grabbed Sahri, and with her strong tail ejected both out of the swirling mass of water.

A male mermaid leaped out of the water, over the dock, and pushed the Fossegrim into the sea. The Fossegrim didn't know what hit him.

The male mermaid is called a Jengy. They wear masks to hide their hideous appearance. They have fought in many battles, but usually keep with their own kind, staying away from the other mermaids from different regions of the world. The Jengy have a kind heart and are always available to lend a helping hand.

Sanna held the Jengy's hand. "Thank you for your help!" Sanna cooed with gratitude.

"It's been a long time since I've seen you!" the Jengy told her. "I was patrolling the waters and just happened to see the Fossegrim."

"I haven't seen a Fossegrim in centuries. Why was he here?" Sanna wondered aloud.

"Lucretia is building a powerful army and wants everyone in her path destroyed!" the Jengy replied

"Are you going to the meeting tonight at Odessa's Island?" Sanna asked.

"We weren't told about a meeting. I will go and tell my people!" the Jengy replied as he turned to go.

"Be careful and swim strong!" lovingly said Sanna.

The Jengy turned back, kissed Sanna on the hand, and swam away quickly.

CHAPTER 17
BACCHUS FOREST

People who enter Bacchus Forest usually don't return. Scuba Jack saw the sign that read "Beware! Go Back!" Despite the warning, he knew he had to get through the forest to reach the Sea Witch's Island.

Scuba Jack walked for ten minutes until he saw an interesting teenage boy hanging from a tree upside down. A dazzling lake sparkled behind him in the bright sunshine.

"Hello!" the teenage boy greeted. "I am just trying out a new exercise regime that will help give me a six pack."

"Hello!" Scuba Jack answered back nervously.

"You realize that anyone entering my forest never returns to civilization?" the teenage boy said.

"Yes, I realize that. But my family is in danger and I need to attend the meeting at the Sea Witch's Island," Scuba Jack responded, sounding anxious.

"Oh, I've heard about you! My name is Henry Reginald Bacchus. They call me a Warlock, but I prefer *Purveyor of Magic*. The title has been passed down for generations. I'm the lucky one to hold the honor this century."

Scuba Jack and Henry looked out over the water and noticed a creature ascending and submerging from the surface of the lake.

"Is that the Loch Ness Monster?" Scuba Jack asked.

Henry threw a cookie toward the creature. The creature retrieved it, tossed the cookie in the air, and then swallowed it.

"Yes, that's Nessie, the Loch Ness Monster" Henry nodded.

Next Scuba Jack noticed a large ape-like creature sitting on a lounge chair next to the water.

"Is that Bigfoot?"

"Yes, he can't stand cameras and paparazzi so he comes here to enjoy some peace and quiet."

Bigfoot let out a loud burp. Then gas escaped his rear end. Henry gasped. "How many times have I told you to stop eating those mushrooms? They don't agree with you! You're sleeping outside tonight!"

Just then both heard loud screeches coming from somewhere high in the air.

"What in the world is that?" Scuba Jack asked.

"The screeching is coming from seven foot bats from the Amazon. They have been asleep for thousands of years, but recently they've been awakened to help Lucretia become more powerful. This is the fourth group of bats I've have seen today!" Henry said as the bats soared over their heads. One swooped down and took the lemonade right out of Big Foots hand!

"Huh?" said Bigfoot.

Then Scuba Jack noticed three doors marked Door Number One, Door Number Two and Door Number Three.

"Where do those doors open to?"

"Elysian Fields, Other Realms, or Hades'
Abode," Henry replied. "The reason why no
one ever returns to civilization is because they
all want to travel to other realms or to Elysian
Fields. Elysian Fields is a magical place, very
much like your heaven!"

A group of waist-high beings began to gather
around Scuba Jack.

"Hello, little fellows, nice to meet you!" Scuba
Jack told them.

In the cutest voice ever the Pukwuggies
replied, "Nice to meet you!"

"These are Pukwuggies, "Henry explained. "They live in Bacchus Forest. They help me keep the peace in the world." Then Henry asked, "Do you know the 11th Choir is following you?"

"Yes, I just met Clem. He seems like a nice guy!" said Scuba Jack.

"I just detected them entering my forest. They're here to help you!"

The Pukwuggies brought a box of pizza to Scuba Jack.

"Thank you, little guys!" Scuba Jack responded, suddenly realizing he was very hungry, indeed!

In the cutest, tiniest, squeakiest voice imaginable the Pukwuggies replied in unison, "You're welcome!"

"You must be on your way, Scuba Jack!" Henry prompted as he bent over and picked up a small rock. He placed the rock on his hand and it levitated.

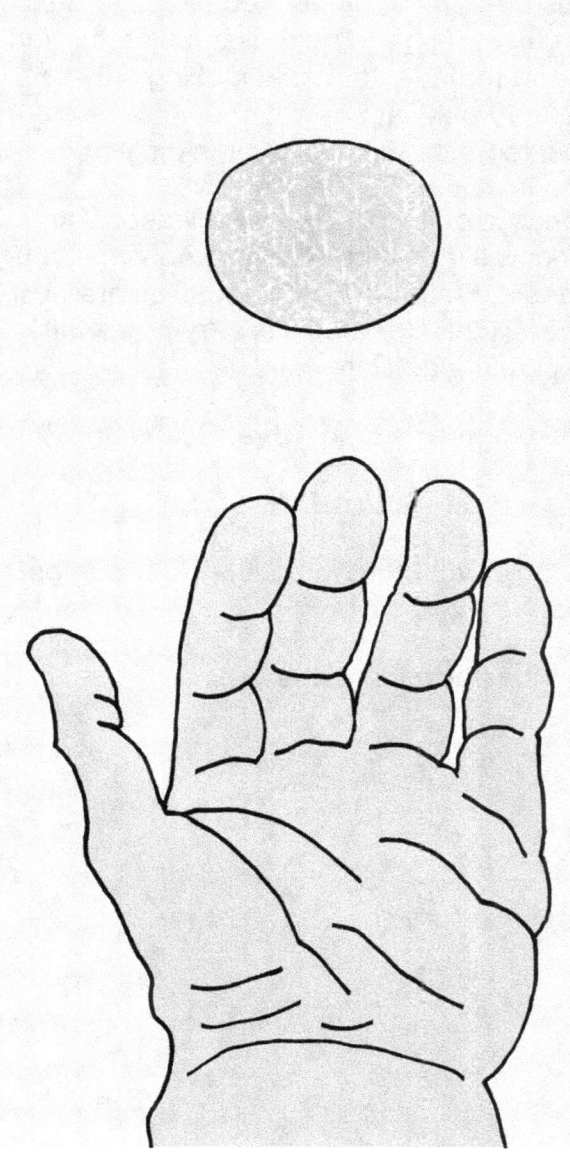

106.

With his other hand he pointed his finger at it in a circular motion. The rock spun faster and faster and turned into a gold looking sphere. Then Henry blew at it and it shot into the sky and created a beautiful fireworks display.

"That trick is definitely a crowd pleaser. The fireworks will let all the Realms know that you have passed through my forest. Be careful of the Sea Witch! Her magic is very powerful!" Henry cautioned. "Farewell!"

The Pukwuggies added, "Bye, Scuba Jack!"

"Wish me luck!" Scuba Jack said,

"Luck, luck, and more luck!" the Pukwuggies chirped.

And Scuba Jack was gone

CHAPTER 18

DINNER WITH
THE SEA WITCH

The Sea Witch had two fumbling lizard assistants who helped her with daily chores and preparing spells. The lizards were named Tolliver and Otis. One day they were sunning themselves on a lovely little rock: the next day they worked for the grouchiest witch on the planet. One of the lizards was turned into a human, while the other lizard was attached to his head.

The Sea Witch had a magical chair that could fly in the air. No, she didn't have a broom like other witches; she had a comfy chair to ride upon. This made dusting much easier.

"Start sweeping the floors!" as she scolded her two assistants.

Just the sound of her voice sent chills up their spines. She made them so scared they ran into the closed door.

"Can't you do anything right?" she screamed.

"Sorry, my lady! We will get right on that and make the floors look new again!" nervously replied Tolliver.

Just then a fly landed on Tolliver's nose. Otis stuck out his tongue and slurped it right off of his nose.

"Stop eating my snacks!" yelled Tolliver.

"Get to work!" yelled the Sea Witch. Our company will be here soon!"

Tolliver and Otis placed a large table in the water for the meeting. Around the table would sit mermaids from each region of the world.

"Set the table, you fools!"

Tolliver and Otis were so frightened of the Sea Witch they ran right into her!

"You fools, I will turn you into a slimy worm. Would you like that? Then a bird could eat you in one gulp!" scoffed Odessa.

"No, my lady. There won't be any need for turning us into worms. We will tidy up and make the island look lovely. By the way, you look very lovely today. Did you do something different with your hair," asked Otis.

"You know my hair is the same. Don't try to butter me up with kindness. I know you're just saying that so I don't turn you into a ghastly, smelly worm!"

ChAPTER 19
The MerMaiD King aND QUEENS ArriVE!

Scuba Jack saw the entrance to the Sea Witch's Island. He knew that he needed to be brave as he entered through the rock doorway!

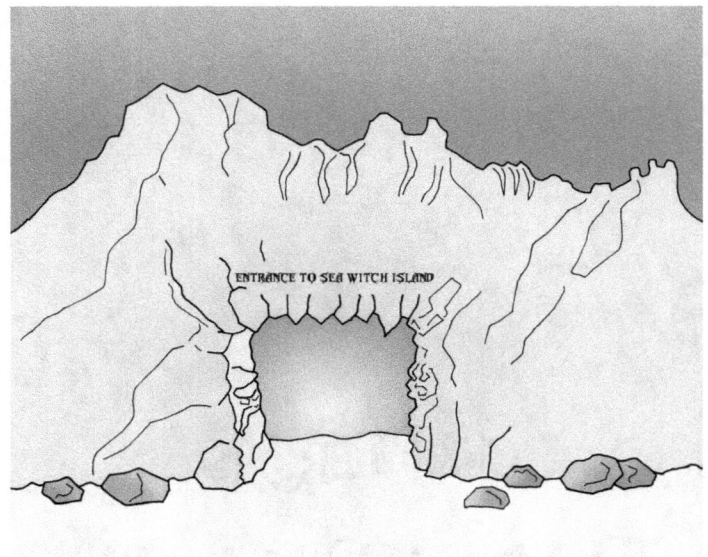

Through the doorway was the Sea Witch's Island. The moon was just about full and the meeting was about to take place.

"I must do this for Sahri and my daughter Jewel. I must get them to listen to me! Well, here goes!" Scuba Jack climbed onto the island and softly opened the door. He walked through the Sea Witch's house which was full of jars filled with bat wings, eyeballs, herbs and spices. A large wooden table sat in the middle of the room. The *Book of Life* sat in the center of the table. It was a spell book that helped her to conjure anything she desired. The page was open to a spell—Memory Loss!

"Memory loss?" Scuba Jack thought to himself. "Maybe Odessa wants the mermaids to forget about the meeting? Maybe she is working with Lucretia?"

A stuffed black cat sat next to the book. It looked as though it was guarding the book. Next to the cat was a crystal ball. Lights moved within the globe and reflected the room with beautiful colors. Just then the door burst open and Tolliver and Otis noticed an intruder snooping around Odessa's secret magic tools.

"What are you doing in here?" asked Tolliver

"I was invited to the meeting and I got lost?"

"The meeting is through that door," replied Otis.

Scuba Jack opened the door quietly and listened to meeting. He wanted to enter at the perfect moment.

"We're here today to discuss the events that have taken place in the world. All the Elemental Realms, along with the Elemental Queen and the Dragon King, need to unite and join forces to rid the world of Lucretia and her army of smelly birds!" Odessa commanded.

Just then the Jengy appeared, uninvited, to attend the meeting.

"What are you doing here?" the Sea Witch asked suspiciously.

"We fought side by side during wars but were cast aside because of our appearance. We aren't interested in your wealth or beauty. We are peaceful people who have been ridiculed and shunned. Our hearts are pure and forgiving. We have forgiven all of you," sternly responded the Jengy.

"You were not shunned!" the King of the Brazilian Mermaids countered. "You wanted to leave our kind! You wanted nothing to do with us and made that perfectly clear when we were fighting Hades and his evil army."

"My people didn't know that Hades was causing havoc. If we did, we would have come to your aid!" the Jengy responded.

"Enough—both of you!" the Sea Witch scolded. "The Elemental Queen wants us to meet her at Atlas' Domain. She needs every kingdom to attend!"

"We will be there, my lady," another Queen promised.

Just then Scuba Jack jumped onto the meeting table. "Please, just hear me out! I know I'm not invited, but I need your help to rid the world of Lucretia and her army of birds. I found all the golden apples and put them in the seal. It opened and inside were three dragon eggs. I delivered them to the Dragon King."

"The seal has been opened?" another mermaid queen asked nervously.

"That only happens when the world is in grave danger!" another queen confirmed.

"Did you know about this, Odessa? Or are you keeping things from us?" the Scottish Queen asked.

"No, I did not know this! Hmmm, why would they keep this information from me? You were NOT invited and need to leave my Island now!" Odessa told Scuba Jack angrily.

Odessa and her chair raised out of the water. Scuba Jack knew he needed to get out of there fast. The Star link wasn't going to work on her island! So HE RAN!!!!!!!

Odessa followed him from behind while sitting in her chair. Scuba Jack ran into her house looking for the door that led to Bacchus Forest while Odessa circled around him and the entire room. She circled him faster and faster on the outside wall of the room which made Scuba Jack dizzy.

Tolliver and Otis watched from outside with fear. They wanted to help Scuba Jack but knew Odessa would turn them into a worm or something worse.

Odessa began to cast a spell.

> "May greeted friends be welcome here,
> People unknown should have great fear.
> Those who without welcome have crossed this floor,
> Shall live with me forevermore."

With that, Odessa blew magic dust into Scuba Jack's face. She circled him faster and faster which made Scuba Jack dizzy.

Scuba Jack started to sway and back and forth. He noticed Odessa's crystal witch's ball on the table and was staring at the light inside that illuminated it.

Odessa yelled, "Don't touch that! Evil attracts to its light, enters inside, and gets stuck there for all eternity!"

Scuba Jack, getting dizzier and dizzier, began to lose his balance. Accidentally, he knocked the witch's ball off the table and it landed on the ground with a loud crash, smashing into a million pieces.

Scuba Jack fell to the floor and was out cold. Black shadowy figures flew out of the shattered glass. Their screams and cries sent shivers up the spine. They engulfed Odessa and launched her out the stained glass window behind her.

Just then globes of small lights entered through the broken window. Ever so gently, they raised Scuba Jack from the ground. Unfortunately they misjudged the opening and Scuba Jack hit his head on the window *(doink!)* but, he was still out cold. The fairies continued to carry him toward his most important destination: home.

CHAPTER 20

SCUBA JACK RETURNS HOME
TO A DESTROYED
MAJESTIC HARBOR

The fairies delivered Scuba Jack to his home. He awoke, looked through his binoculars and saw all the devastation that occurred. He also noticed eggs in nests everywhere. "This is not good!" he sighed

"You need to be at the meeting at Atlas' Domain," a voice said from behind him.

Scuba Jack turned around. He saw Clem. "It's good to see you!" he said.

"It's good to be seen!" Clem replied. "I wasn't sure you would make it out of there alive!"

"Scuba Jack!" The voice was Professor Galaxy's. "I have been looking all over for you! Lucretia has destroyed everything and she has Paco!"

It was Clem who answered. "Your friend is not your friend anymore. He belongs to Lucretia. I am sorry boys, but you can't get him back!"

"We never back down from a challenge, do we, Scuba Jack?" Professor Galaxy said.

"Nope, we never do!"

Clem asked, "Do I need to remind you that what you are about to do is dangerous?"

"Nope! But you'll be there to help, right?" Scuba Jack smiled.

Professor Galaxy leaned over to ask, "Who is this guy?"

"He is with the 11th Choir, or you can call him a Watcher, or you can call him a Grigori. Long story short, he protects the universe."

"Oh good! We always need protection. He should come in handy."

CHAPTER 21

LET'S GET OUR BFF, Paco!

"I brought some things with me Scuba Jack" said the Professor.

"What kind of things?"

"A flame thrower and some pepper."

Together they said, "Scrambled EGGS!"

"Honey, I'll be home soon!" Scuba Jack said. "The Professor and I are going to save Paco! Let's go Professor! I'm hungry!"

Meanwhile, Paco was feeding Lucretia grapes one by one.

"Would you like something to drink, too, Lucretia?"

"No, but my feathers need to be fluffed and cleaned!"

"Sure. I would love to do that for you, Lucretia!" Paco replied obediently.

Scuba Jack and Professor Galaxy discovered Lucretia's nest area. There were eggs everywhere! "Have you ever seen so many eggs?" Professor Galaxy whispered.

"Look! It's Paco!" Scuba Jack whispered back. "You go that way. I'll go this way."

Scuba Jack and The Professor approached the nest from behind. They quietly grabbed Paco and put tape around his beak. They tied a rope around him and said, "Don't say a word or your lady is going to become a soft feather pillow!"

"Stop! I will give you money, I will give you power! I will make you second in command!" commanded Lucretia.

"Um, let me think about it! That would be a big, fat, NO!" said the Professor.

"That's a NO for me too!" sarcastically said Scuba Jack.

The three jumped off the nest. Professor Galaxy yelled really loud, "I've been waiting a long, long time for this! He grabbed onto a vine and swung across the field like a super hero!

With a click of the button, flames shot out of the flamethrower. It cracked open the eggs, and began to cook them.

Professor Galaxy really seemed to be enjoying himself until Scuba Jack interrupted.

"OK. OK. Really good job. Put down the flame thrower?"

"What? I can't hear you! This flame thrower is really awesome, don't you think????"

Scuba Jack clicked the button, turning off the flamethrower. "OK. Enough! That is a lot of scrambled eggs. We can't possibly eat them all. Not to mention that we need to reverse the spell that I put on poor Paco."

"First things first......Let's eat!" the Professor said.

Scuba Jack nodded as if to say, "Yeah, sure!"

"Let's not forget the pepper!" the Professor said.

The two dined on fabulous scrambled eggs sprinkled with pepper.

"I'm stuffed!"

"Me, too!"

"OK, Here's the wand and here's the book," the Professor said, pulling them out .

"Let me see if there's a spell to reverse love?" After a few seconds, he said, "OK, found it. Here we go! It says that I need to say this ten times…

A spell was cast,
Now make it past.
Remove it now,
Don't ask me how.
Please let it be!

The spell worked like a charm.

Paco tried to talk but his mouth was taped shut.

The Professor laughed and freed Paco's beak. "Here you go, little guy!"

"What's going on?" Paco asked.

"Long story! But you were in love with an evil Pelican named Lucretia! You were feeding her grapes and fluffing her feathers. It wasn't pretty!"

"Professor, Scuba Jack……I am not feeling so well. My tummy doesn't feel very well"

Paco let out a large burp! "Oh, I feel much better! Well, maybe not!"

Scuba Jack and Professor Galaxy knew that the greenish color on his face could only mean one thing. They were both going to be victims of disgusting, smelly, slimy vomit sauce.

"No Paco, NOOOOOOO!" cried the Professor.

Paco opened his beak as wide as he could and projectile vomit covered both Scuba Jack and the Professor.

"I am guessing by the smell, Paco, that you had sardines for breakfast?" asked Scuba Jack.

"You know that sardines don't agree with you!" added the Professor.

"He even got it in my ear!" said Scuba Jack.

"We need to take a shower!" said the Professor

"Sorry, my friends! I didn't mean to throw up on you! Sometimes it just happens when I get nervous. Thank you for saving me from that evil Lucretia!" said Paco.

"That is what best friends are for!" said the Professor.

ChaPTER 22

The ELEMENTaL QUEEN PULLS TogeTheR an ARMy

Mermaids, fairies, elves, leprechauns, Spell Casters, Pukwuggies, and Henry Reginald Bacchus came to help the Elemental Queen. The Dragon King brought his six Dragons to aid in this monumental task.

"My friends, thank you for coming to the aid of the humans and our planet. They need our help to rid the world of Lucretia's evil plan. To do this, we must turn back time two days prior to when things were normal and peaceful. We must combine all our magic now to help Atlas turn his mighty globe back two rotations."

The dragons began to jump with joy, getting ready to aid Atlas and use their strength to reverse the earth's rotation. The Dragon King's mermaids had a hard time just holding their harnesses to keep the excited dragons under control.

Meanwhile back at Majestic Harbor..............

Mermaid hybrids were getting rid of all of the birds at Majestic Harbor.

The hybrids could easily shift from sea to land. Their legs sprouted and their strength was incredible, and their speed was lightning fast. Nothing could beat their incredible powers. They possessed immortal strength. In other words, the birds and eggs were toast!

CHAPTER 23

A LARGE STONE DOOR OPENED

The Elemental Queen walked into a large room followed by her many realms.

"Hello Atlas! We are here to help! We must turn the world back two days!" she said.

"I will try, Your Majesty" Atlas responded.

Everyone in the great room put their hands in the air. Just then two hundred Watchers entered the room. "We're here to help!" Clem informed her.

"Release the dragons!" the Elemental Queen commanded.

The six dragons flew around the world in the opposite direction that it was spinning. Their combined power and force would help turn the globe in the opposite direction.

The dragons had a hard time flying in the wind they were creating. It was so strong that the younger dragons had to fly behind the older dragons. Atlas used every last bit of his strength trying to stop the earth from rotating.

Scuba Jack pulled out his spell book and began reciting a spell over and over!

> Turn back the clock
>
> Make time stand still—
>
> Two days prior,
>
> This be your will.
>
> Rid this world of birds that are evil,
>
> Stop all this destruction and upheaval.
>
> Please let it be!

The six dragons fell to the ground exhausted. Incredible strength and magic was needed to do such a miraculous feat! Breathing very heavily, one of the dragons got up and screeched a really loud cry as if to summon the other five dragons who were resting for a moment. The six dragons all got up and stood side by side and jumped into the air. Again, the force was too much and they fell to the floor exhausted! Just then Odessa the Sea Witch walked into the room and said, "Let me offer my assistance! Dragons, you must use all your might! Atlas, please help us and use all your strength to stop the rotation!" commanded Odessa.

The dragons got into a ready position and leaped into the air.   They flew with all their might and roared as they successfully circled the earth one rotation. Then they circled the earth a second time. Then, suddenly the earth stopped spinning. Atlas' eyes grew wide!

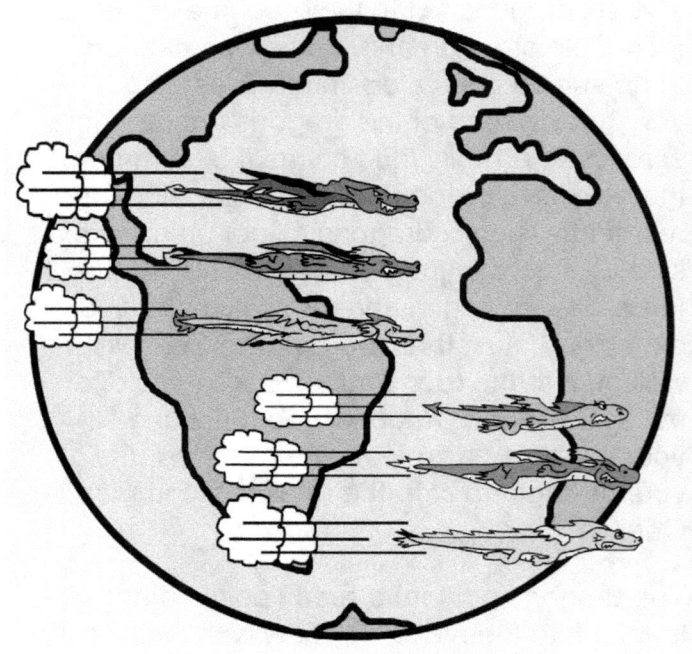

"It worked!" a Spell Caster yelled.

"Go and get Lucretia. Bring her to me!" the Elemental Queen said, summoning Henry Reginald Bacchus.

"Yes, Your Majesty!"

Poof! Henry Reginald Bacchus was gone!

Henry returned within one minute with Lucretia.

"You have caused a great deal of harm to the universe! I hereby sentence you to an eternity at the Kingdom of the Dragon King. These six fierce Dragons will watch over you, ensuring your good behavior," commanded the Elemental Queen.

"Dear Atlas, please rotate the earth for me!" fondly asked the Queen.

"My pleasure, my lady!" answered Atlas.

The earth rotated in its normal direction from the two days prior to all the destruction. Everything was back to normal.

CHAPTER 24

Majestic Harbor Returns to Normal

Scuba Jack, Professor Galaxy and Paco returned to Scuba Jack's dock.

"Well, we did it! We saved the world again!" Scuba Jack smiled.

"Yes, we did!" Professor Galaxy confirmed.

"Thanks again for saving me from that awful Lucretia!" Paco sighed.

Two mermaids swam to the dock. Sahri walked out to greet them.

"Honey, this is my sister, Sanna. She saved Jewel and I from a whirlpool and a Fossegrim!" Sahri said.

"A Fosse what?" Scuba Jack asked.

"I've heard a lot about you, Scuba Jack!" Sanna pulled herself from the water and gave Scuba Jack a kiss on the cheek.

"I would like to introduce you to the love of my life, Santi!" Sanna pulled off his mask. Scuba Jack bent down to shake his hand. "I couldn't have saved Sahri and Jewel without him!" Sanna said proudly.

"It's nice to meet you!" Scuba Jack responded.

Santi smiled because Scuba Jack didn't seem to mind his appearance and was thankful for all his efforts.

"It's nice to meet you! I have known Sahri for a long time. You're a lucky human!" Santi replied.

Just then Scuba Jack noticed Clem walking up the dock.

"Oh, hello Clem! It's nice to see you again!" said Scuba Jack.

"Honey, I have been meaning to tell you," Sahri said excitedly. "But you were really busy saving the world and all. We're having another baby!"

"Do you want to know what it is?" Clem asked.

"Yes, I would!" Sahri said.

"It's a girl!"

"I want to name her Jacksanna, after her father and my sister." Sahri added lovingly.

"Honey, that's beautiful!" Scuba Jack said as he kissed Sahri on the cheek. Then he added, "Hey, I am beat! It's hard work saving the world!"

As they all said good night, Clem said, "I'll be seeing you again, Jack!"

"I hope so!" Jack replied, smiling and shaking Clem's hand.

CHAPTER 25
A FAIRY VISIT

That night as Scuba Jack slept he felt a tug on his arm. He opened his eyes to see two fairies.

"Hey, what are you doing here?" sleepily said Scuba Jack.

"We wanted to give you a gift for saving the world! We want to give you this dream box.

"It foretells the future. All you need to do is write a question you want answered by the universe."

"Ok, said Scuba Jack, still half a sleep!

"We knew you were tired so we wrote a question for you!" one of the fairies said excitedly.

"The answer to the question will come to you tonight in your dreams!" said the other fairy.

"We asked the dream box what your next adventure will be," answered the Fairy.

"Oh, that's awesome!" Scuba Jack said. He rolled over and pulled the blanket over his head.

Scuba Jack was in a deep, peaceful sleep when he abruptly sat up in bed and yelled, "Crystal Skulls? What in the world are those? I am going **where**?"

www.ingramcontent.com/pod-product-compliance
Lightning Source LLC
Chambersburg PA
CBHW071302130626
46556CB00003B/1436